For Ann

Acknowledgments

"Dancing on the Edge of the World," online and in print in *To the Stars Through Difficulties: A Kansas Renga* (2012)

"Driving U. S. 36," online in *Prairie Poetry* (2002)

"Dark Dove Descending," *Kansas Stories* (1989)

"Night Sounds," *The Flint Hills Review* (2004); reprinted online in "150 Kansas Poems" and in print in *Begin Again: 150 Kansas Poems* (2011)

"Primordial Prayer," *Angel Face* (2006)

"Homing In," *The Left Bank Review* (1998)

"Auspicious Day," *The Laughing Dog* (2005)

"My Advice," *The Dos Passos Review* (Spring 2005); reprinted online in *Kansas Poets & Poetry Archive* and as Kansas Arts Commission Ad Astra Poetry Project #42 (2009)

"The Baseball Mitt," *The Tampa Review* (1997)

"Vespers," *Angel Face* (2005)

"Evening Callers," online as a winner of Ad Astra Poetry Contest #8 (2009)

"The Lap of Lechery," *Arete: The Journal of Sports Literature* (Spring 1986)

"Premonition," *The Laughing Dog* (2005)

"The Notice," *The Quarterly* (Spring 1993)

"All This Moving Apart," *Angel Face* (2005); reprinted online in *Kansas Poets & Poetry Archive*

"A Parable of Plumbing," *Hurākan* (1998)

"Robins Keep Their Secrets," online in "150 Kansas Poems" and in print in *Begin Again: 150 Kansas Poems* (2011)

"The Red Stone Mystery," *Voodoo Souls Quarterly* (2000)

"Lost and Found," online in "150 Kansas Poems. 2013: Poem of the Week" (July 15)

Grateful acknowledgment is made to the editors of the above publications. Several works have been revised for their appearance in this book. Many thanks to all who offered valuable time and advice to make these poems and stories and this book better, including Ann Meats, Jo McDougall, Denise Low, Bill Sheldon, John Meats, Kane Leins, Charles Cagle, Suzanne Lindsay, Gordon Lish, and Naomi Shihab Nye. Any errors or lapses in taste or judgment are mine.

I would also like to express a special thanks to Denise Low, who with Thomas Pecore Weso, created Mammoth Publications as a vehicle for writers of Kansas and beyond.

Contents

Foreword

Many writers owe a great debt to Stephen Meats' insight as poetry editor of *The Midwest Quarterly*. But readers, too, have benefitted from Meats' good eye, and his first book of poems, *Looking for the Pale Eagle* (Woodley Press, 1993), has served as a tutorial in seeing the world with fresh sight.

In the title poem of *Pale Eagle*, the speaker sees "for the thousandth / or ten thousandth time" a blackbird. He notes the red wing for which the bird is named, but something else as well: "From below its crimson epaulet / a glint of yellow winked at me." That moment is instructive. We call it a *red winged* blackbird, and in so doing we notice, as a matter of duty, that red patch on its wing. Meats suggests, however, that we must look beyond the name we have given this bird to see it in all its parts. For the poem's persona, that moment is an epiphany when, "Sunlight sang / across the ditch water." The poem ends with the admonition, "All you had to do / was look—and look—and keep on looking." That poem and those that follow serve as a primer for observing the world. Further, poems like the three-word "Coastline"—

s i l e n t
i n l e t s
l i s t e n

—demonstrate that the same hard look must be given to the language chosen to reflect one's observations of the world. Meats' poems are examples of Coleridge's notion of "the best words in their best order."

Consequently, many readers have longed for the next Stephen Meats collection.

The satisfying outcome of that wait is *Dark Dove Descending and Other Parables* in which Meats continues to demonstrate how to see with new eyes the familiar world and how to write about what one sees.

The poems in this collection, as were those in *Pale Eagle*, are often focused on epiphanies arising from everyday detail, on tightly constructed lines, and on the music of those lines, as in "Premonition":

> I did not notice you had put
> the paper down and slipped away
> until I looked up and saw the wrinkles
> relaxing on your palm tree pillow
> and the lamplight pooling
> on your empty chair.

Furthermore, Meats' carefully chosen metaphors allow us to see the usual in new ways, or give voice to the familiar that we did not, until now, have voice for. In "Driving U.S. 36," Meats writes,

> Bluffs stick their bony knees and elbows
> into the creeks that beat beneath the bridges
> like rhythms of an ancient chant.

That initial metaphor, the observation of the "bony" bluffs, leads into the simile that takes us to the heart of human existence, and a significant theme in this book, a confrontation with time, that Meats calls, in "Night Sounds," "some inevitable / unimaginable what" and in "Primordial Prayer," "the face of that inscrutable intent / that gives life only to take it away." Thus, while Meats laments in one piece,

> the distance we cannot cross
> between this lie of language
> and the truth of dirt and branch
> and bird and bone,

his poems continue to come as close as any to spanning that void and addressing anew our world and how we live in it.

The stories, which often take on fabulist or parable-like qualities, are likewise concerned with epiphanies arising organically from the everyday. For example, the young boy in the title story realizes in his sixth year that his older brother truly hates him, and the slightly older boy in "The Lap of Lechery" encounters his first drunken adult in his baseball coach, who is also one of the first pair of adults the boy witnesses having sex (forgotten memories themselves an epiphany triggered by the discovery of a bloody T-shirt).

From the initially quotidian depiction of "The Baseball Mitt," to the startlingly dream-like sequence of "Homing In" (with its climax in a bookstore called The Hopeful Reader), whether writing in a realistic or surrealistic vein, Meats brings the same hard-eyed craftsmanship to his fiction that informs his poetry, each story containing a satori-like realization best described in "Lost and Found":

> "We turn west now, having found what we didn't even know we were looking for, toward the comfort of familiar ground and home."

Therein lies the strength of Meats' poetry and prose, which not only show us that which we might not see on our own, but give words to those things we know but know not how to say. With *Dark Dove Descending,* readers and writers continue under Stephen Meats' tutelage to envision the world with fresh eyes.

William Sheldon

Dark Dove Descending and Other Parables

Dancing on the Edge of the World

Seventeen miles south of Concordia
in a small stand of trees off old
Highway 81 there was once a wayside
drinking fountain, a single pipe rising
out of the ground from which welled up
perpetually the coldest clearest water.
It's long since been effaced
by the four-lane, but fifty years ago,
for restless teenagers in town, to drive out
to the fountain of a summer night,
to watch the lights of the safe and familiar
streets disappear in the rearview mirror,
was to venture close to the edge of a dark
yet beckoning unknown, where,
balanced on the very rim of our world,
we would tune the car radios to KOMA
in Oklahoma City, and with the Top Forty
pouring down from a limitless sky,
drink of the cold artesian flow
and dance for our lives.

Driving U. S. 36

Northwest Kansas.
Land of limestone outcroppings.
Where the bones show through.
Where wood was once so scarce
fence posts were cut from stone.
North wind keeps a constant hand on the wheel.
Bluffs stick their bony knees and elbows
into the creeks that beat beneath the bridges
like the rhythms of an ancient chant:
Running Turkey, Buffalo, Prairie Dog,
Minnesappa: Cheyenne for black water.
Willow and cottonwood grow
sparse along their winding threads.
Yucca spikes up through pasture grass.
Old snow survives in the shadows of culverts
and deep between rows of winter wheat,
bright green against dingy white,
the fields of spring shrugging off
winter's shabby garment.

Dark Dove Descending

A kid just naturally looks up to his older brother. I was no different. I admired Kenny because he could throw a baseball all the way from the light pole to the front porch, because he could wiggle his ears, because he had permanent teeth—in other words, because he was my brother. That's why it was a shock when I realized when I was six that Kenny hated me. This is no exaggeration. It wasn't that he just didn't like me. He hated me, and not for anything I had ever done to him, but for taking up his space, breathing his air, for being born—transgressions I could never atone for.

It was in the spring of 1951, the year that three months of continuous rains turned the normally mild Republican River into a two-mile-wide torrent that left north central Kansas devastated.

The first storm roared in from the southwest on a Friday night in early March. Kenny and I were awakened about two in the morning by abrupt rain battering the tin roof of our four-room rented farmhouse. We heard our dad dress and go out.

Through the bedroom window we watched his lantern slant through the stiff dark as he went to close the chicken house against the storm.

By seven o'clock Saturday when Dad left for his job at

the seed warehouse in town, the rain had stopped but the sky was solid slate. As soon as my brother and I ran out the backdoor after breakfast, we heard the sound. The usually dry creek that ran past our place was bank-full with violent run-off from the night's rain.

Neither of us said a word. We climbed the three-strand barbwire fence at the gatepost and raced straight across the small pasture toward the elms that lined the creek. The wind and rain had laid the winterbrown grass down slick to the ground like wet hair plastered to a child's skull.

The flooding creek was magnificent. Kenny and I stood silently fascinated by the frothed and tossing brown water, and by its voice that we listened to not with our ears so much as with our eyes, the soles of our feet, the surface of our skin.

My brother picked up a stick and tossed it into the water. We watched it dance down the roiling creek and out of sight around the bend. I couldn't believe how fast it moved.

"I bet it's deep!" Kenny said next to my ear. He had to shout to make himself heard. "Let's see how deep! Find a stick!" His face was as wild and urgent as the surface of the creek.

I found a dead limb about six feet long that the wind had blown down. I tried to hand it to my brother because I knew he claimed the right to do every exciting thing first and every odious thing last. This time, though, he surprised me.

"You do it!" he shouted. I don't think he could have foreseen what happened next. After all, he hadn't made it rain, he hadn't made the creek flood.

I stood at the edge of the water and leaned out over the creek. I thrust the stick as straight down into the swift water as I could. One second I was concentrating on probing for the bottom, and the next thing I felt was a breath-sucking shock as I hit the cold water face first.

I was driven deep into the creek by the powerful current. The world went abruptly silent. My hands and knees brushed the bottom and I somersaulted lazily over onto my back. I opened my eyes, and all I could see was a distant muddy luminescence that diminished as it descended toward me. I felt calm even though I had never been in water deeper than a stock tank and had no idea how to swim. I did not struggle. It was like I was flying. I was suddenly free of gravity and could feel the current buoying me along. Without even thinking I spread my arms out like wings, closed my eyes, and gave myself up to the rushing water.

I wasn't aware I was floating to the top until my face broke the surface. I was thirty yards or more downstream and already out of sight around the bend. I had been instinctively holding my breath and let out a burst of air like a cry. My right hand brushed dead weeds that were trailing in the current along the bank and I grabbed hold almost by reflex. Not until then did I feel any fear.

The current swung me in toward the bank, and I shouted for my brother. "Kenny! Help me! I'm down here! Help!" Then the weeds broke loose and the current pulled me under again. This time I struggled and swallowed water. The sensation was sharp and suffocating like a large rock lodged under my breast bone.

I came up choking and managed to grab the stalk of a

sumac bush as I was swept past it. I pulled myself half out of the water. My brother was nowhere in sight. "Ken! Help!" I suddenly felt weak and cold and began to cry. "Help me, Kenny, help me!"

I couldn't understand why he didn't come. For what seemed like a long time, I lay there half out of the water with my cheek in the mud sobbing and shivering and clutching the little bush.

I must have lost consciousness then because the next thing I knew my mother had me by the jacket collar and was dragging me face downward through the mud up the bank. She was small herself, not really much bigger than I was, and my water-soaked clothes must have nearly doubled my weight, and yet she snatched me up as if I were a helium balloon and ran with me in her arms across the pasture.

I don't think she knew I was alive until she got me to the house. She dumped me roughly on the linoleum floor and shook my face with both her hands as she knelt beside me. I opened my eyes and she cried out, "Jesusjesusthankgod you stupid little shit!" and hit me twice in the face with her open hand and then hugged my head to her breast as she wept. Then she stripped me and wrapped me in a comforter and set me blue and trembling in Dad's overstuffed chair by the oil stove in the living room. She tried to telephone Dad at the seed warehouse but the lines were down because of the storm.

When the warmth finally began to revive me, I opened my eyes. Through the kitchen door I saw my brother sitting at the table. He had been there quietly eating saltines with apple butter the entire time Mom was trying to rouse me.

The look he gave me was like a sharp, unexpected push from behind. As young as I was, I understood what that look meant. It was his declaration of the war between us. And there was something else there, too, but I started to cry before I saw what it was.

My mother heard me and came immediately. "What's the matter, Paulie? Tell me what's wrong." Kenny stopped chewing but the expression in his eyes didn't change.

I shook my head no. "I'm ok," I said.

When Dad got home that evening, Mom told him what had happened. "We might have lost him if Kenny hadn't come to the house right away," Mom said. Dad roughed up Kenny's hair with his hand and hugged his head in the crook of his elbow. "Thanks for looking after your little brother, bud. As for you," he said, turning to me, "what in hell were you doing playing around that creek?"

That night the rain kept up a steady ringing on the tin roof as Kenny and I lay without talking in the double bed we shared in the unheated room off the kitchen. I must have been drifting off to sleep because I thought I was under the water like I had been that morning, but it was all going backwards. I kept trying to turn around and ride the current, but something was forcing me to struggle upstream toward the spot where I fell in. The cold shock of hitting the water came back to me, and every muscle I had gave a violent jerk that jolted me wide awake. It's hard to put into words, but it was like my body was trying to remind me of something I didn't want to remember. I felt a suffocating pain rising out of my chest and into my throat. Tears began streaming out of the corners of my eyes, though I wasn't crying.

"Kenny."

"Yeah."

"Why didn't you come when I yelled for you?"

"I didn't hear you."

"Why not?"

He hesitated just a second before he answered. "I already went up to the house to tell Mom you had drownded," he said.

The gloom above the bed seemed to bend down and touch my forehead like the wings of a dark dove descending. My whole life opened up before me like an ominous landscape over which Kenny's slate-gray shadow loomed from somewhere behind me, and I realized that what I wanted but could not have was to fly again through the brown silence at the bottom of the creek—easy and quiet and free forever.

Night Sounds

Sounds hang strangely
in the night air, a noisy quiet
that isolates and amplifies.
Breezes tappling in the cottonwoods,
cicadas rasping up and down,
trucks pounding the distant highway,
cars hissing along the street,
a train two miles away picking up speed,
signaling mile crossings,
its receding wall of sound
like background radiation
fading all the way from creation.

A car door slams and signals what—
arrival or departure. Maybe just routine.
Maybe not. Someone's voice,
a laugh the wind distorts.
Cries, miserable, repetitive,
the only voice the old woman
across the street
has left after her stroke.

My Boston Terrier hovers
in the shadow of a maple's trunk,
head up, ears alert.
I'm standing there too, in the dark,
waiting for him to finish his business
when that strange quality of night sounds
catches in my throat: expectancy.

So much waiting to happen.
Temperature falling toward the dew point.
Sun circling the planet toward morning,
every day working a degree or two
closer to the equator like a string
wound in a spiral around a stick.
Circumstances turning as on a pivot
toward some inevitable
unimaginable what.

Primordial Prayer

Our yellow and white cat is more
than sixteen years old now. When
he isn't sleeping, he totters
through the rooms of the house
and up and down the hallway crying.
His cry is the strongest thing
he has left. A horrific cry.
Visitors react to it with terror.
"What in the hell is that?"
And after we say it's just our old cat,
they ask with sympathy,
"Is he sick? or hurt?"
But we can't explain what is beyond words.
It's as if he puts into his cry
all the life that no longer finds space
in his shriveling husk of a body.
Or maybe it's just his primordial prayer,
the unanswerable question of the betrayed
in the face of that inscrutable intent
that gives life only to take it away.

Fierce Heart

In the field across the street
patches of snow are lacunae
in the solid world
the eye tries to, but can't fill in.
A flock of feeding starlings
pleats and folds
among clumps of grass
the sun draws up
through the snow.
Suddenly a whisper
of translucent wings
and the starlings rise together.
In every mote
of that cloud undulating
across the white sky
a fierce heart beating
200 times a minute.

Homing In

I am trying to find my way home. It should be a simple thing, yet I am utterly at a loss. I am on the eighth level of an empty underground parking garage and have no idea how I got here. I should be able to retrace my steps, but the ramps I can see from where I stand all lead down.

Laughter spirals up one of the ramps behind me. I turn to look and see a dark-haired young woman in a plaid dress walking toward me across the deserted parking area. She is pushing a baby stroller, the double kind, and in the stroller are identical twins. They are naked, and both are grinning open-mouthed toothless drooling grins. Their genitals are fully mature and both have erections.

She takes my hand like we are old friends. I clasp my arm around her waist.

"I can't find my way home," I tell her. She leans her face close to mine and smiles.

"You've gotten below your level," she says. "If you go back up, you'll see your way again."

She points. Sure enough, there is an up-ramp. I feel foolish. Why didn't I see it before? She turns to me and I cup her breasts. Her dress dampens against my palms.

"I'm breast-feeding the twins," she says. "You've made my milk let down, so I'd better go feed them. You can tell they're hungry. Look at those erections. If you had one, I could feed you, too."

She kisses me open-mouthed and deep and her left hand touches my crotch. Desire tightens in my chest but I feel no other stirring. She pushes me teasingly away and laughs. "But we know that won't happen, don't we."

She strollers the twins back down the ramp. I watch over the rail until there is only the echo of her laughter spiraling upward.

I follow the up-ramp she pointed out and emerge from the fluorescent glare of the garage onto a vast asphalt parking lot. The sun stands straight up in the sky.

On the horizon to the east I can see a city skyline, to the north the dark silhouettes of trees, to the west a range of mountains like an approaching storm.

In a shabby strip-center on the south side of the lot is a bookstore. A crudely hand-painted sign above the door says "The Hopeful Reader."

I enter the shop. The bookshelves reach high and the ceiling is obscured by gloom.

I approach the clerk behind the checkout counter. His straight black hair is parted in the middle. His left arm is in a white canvas sling that hides his hand. The sling is clasped with a silver buckle.

"I'm looking for a map to home," I say. He smiles. One of his front teeth is missing.

"Maps to home, Section D-8," the man says. He locks the register and I notice that his right eye doesn't track quite straight. He steps from behind the counter and leads the way.

The narrow center aisle is crossed at odd angles by many other aisles. Voices of customers come from all directions. Some are crying, some whispering, some laughing, some shouting, some singing, but I see no one.

We pass several section signs that seem in no recognizable order. The clerk, who has gotten perhaps a dozen steps ahead, turns into a cross aisle. When I turn after him, I find him blocking my way.

He removes his arm from the sling, and I see why he has kept his left hand hidden. It is not a hand at all but a dark and shriveled claw.

He holds the claw close to my face. "You are responsible for this," he says. "In fact, you are responsible for all my imperfections. And just to make sure you never forget it. . . ."

From the top of his boot he pulls a hunting knife. He cuts the claw off at the wrist and tucks it into my shirt pocket.

Without another word he begins to climb the shelves. I watch until all I can see is the silver buckle glinting in the gloom. I try to climb after, but the books keep shaling under my hands.

Finally, I give up exhausted and try to find my way to the front of the store. The aisles lead away in patternless disorder. Fear tightens around my heart. All the while, voices, voices from all directions, but no one to be seen.

I wander aimlessly through the store. Suddenly the twins from the underground garage toddle out of a cross aisle. They are drooling wide-mouthed toothless wails of grief.

I stoop and hug them to me. "There, there, boys, don't cry. What's wrong?"

"Our mother's dead," their baby voices sob in unison.

"Dead?" I cry in disbelief. "How can she be dead? I just left you a few minutes ago!"

"She fell and rolled down into the dark and there's no one to feed us and we're very very hungry." They show me their erections. The blood of the severed claw in my shirt pocket is cold against my skin.

I feel sudden stirrings of a strange desire. A wave of purpose comes over me. The tightness in my chest lets go. I see what I must do. I unbutton my shirt and suckle the twins until their bellies bulge and their erections shrivel. Once they are fast asleep, I lay them in cardboard boxes and close the lids. When I turn to put the boxes on a shelf, I see that I am at the front of the store.

Customers are lining up at the checkout counter to pay for their stacks of books. The register is locked but I see that my claw will fit the lock perfectly. I open the register and begin to check them out.

Auspicious Day

Today
the first flocking
of blackbirds—
grackle, cowbird,
redwing, the
inevitable starling—
in the gums,
the oaks,
the sycamores,
the gaudy field
of sunflowers.

Tonight
the moon
will not remain
quietly in the corner
of the room
but will step
from the shadows
and touching me
lightly on the shoulder
radiantly
turn the year
toward autumn.

My Advice

You say you want to find yourself. You'll need
a chunk of gravel. Drive any rocked road
in Kansas and you'll hear pieces by the hundreds

knocking in your wheel wells. For once, stop
and get out of the car. Take a minute to look
at the sky—flat bottomed clouds shadowing

the pastures. You'll hear the meadowlark
on the fence post before you see him fly.
Pick up your piece of gravel. If you're far

off the main route, a handful of chat, or even
road sand will do. Cup it in your palm while your
tires hum away the miles on the asphalt highway.

In the next town, warm it in your pocket and stay
a while to look at the faces and listen to the talk
as you drink your coffee at the café counter.

Then take it home with you and right away
put it in your garden or your flower box or drop
it in the driveway. It doesn't really matter.

The Baseball Mitt

When the boy's name was drawn in May for one of the city league teams, his father would not permit him to play, saying that at nine the boy was old enough to start helping in the shop in which the father repaired farm machinery.

The mother had taken the son's side. The arguments went on through May and into June. The father whipped the boy twice for talking back and even threatened to hit the mother to get her to leave him alone about it.

"How you think it makes him feel working all the time and them other boys playing?"

"We settled this before. He's got work to do in the shop. It's time he learned life ain't play."

"I think you don't want him to have no fun. Cause you never had none growing up. Well, don't take your life out on him."

That's when he shook a clinched fist at her. She shut up then, but her accusation stung. The father had always been certain that his way for the boy was the right way. Now, he suddenly saw the truth of what his wife said. He was starting to work his son like his own father had worked him. And he had whipped his son, too, something he had vowed he would never do. His own father had whipped him until he could stand no more and ran away before he was fifteen.

The father thought of the boys from the families in the better parts of town, where the streets were curbed and paved and the lawns stretched out like carpet before the houses. They played ball instead of working and yet they had a better life than he could give his family. This struck him forcefully. Why shouldn't his son have the same chance as those boys? He was good as them.

The father decided then to let his son play. But it was three more days before he could bring himself to tell the boy. Right after breakfast on Tuesday in the last week of June, while they were finishing a valve job on a tractor, the father asked the boy if the team still practiced during the season or if they only played the games.

"They practice Wednesday evenings and play the games on Friday," the boy said. This he knew well because he slipped off after work to watch his team whenever he could. He did not lift his eyes from the thin film of oil he was applying to the gasket.

"I been thinking," said the father. "When I was your age I never got to play ball because I had to work." He saw the boy's neck stiffen and realized that his son did not want to hear again about his hard life.

"But now I'm thinking," he hurried on, "maybe I missed something. So I decided, maybe if I watched you practice with the team, and it looked okay, maybe you could play."

The boy listened with no change of expression. He looked away from his father out the door of shop. It was harvest time. The light wavered above the graveled alley in morning air that was already hot.

The father did not understand his silence. "Well, you

want to play or not?"

"Yes," the boy said, still looking away. Tears stung his eyes. He ran out of the shop and into the house so his father would not see him cry.

"I thought you'd be happy about it," the father shouted after him as the screen door slammed. He shook his head and continued carefully adjusting the valve tolerances.

In a few minutes, the boy returned. His cheeks were scrubbed and his nose was red, but his face was calm. He went to the work bench and began cleaning the valve cover with a kerosene soaked rag.

"You change your mind about playing?"

"No."

"So, you want to go to the practice tomorrow?"

"Yes," the boy said and handed the valve cover to his father. At that moment the mother appeared in the shop door.

"You want something?" the father asked.

"You say he could play ball?"

"That's what I said. You decide now he oughtn't to?"

The mother looked at the father for a time. "There's no taking this back, you know."

"Ain't you got work to do?" the father asked her. She turned then and went back to the house.

Next evening father and son walked to the ball diamond. The father walked as he always did, with his right shoulder thrust a little forward. The boy stayed half a step behind. They did not talk. The boy asked the coach if he could still get on the team. The coach welcomed him, but cautioned that he might not play much with only two weeks left in the season. Then the coach called the boys for batting practice.

The father watched from the unpainted wooden bleachers. When the boy's turn came to bat, he stood on the right-handed side of the plate and gripped the bat cross-handed. He swung awkwardly at the first two pitches and missed. The coach walked to home plate and turned the boy around to the left-handed side and moved the bat to his left shoulder. The coach put his arms around the boy from behind and showed him how to grip the bat and step and swing. When he talked to the boy, he let his arm rest on the boy's shoulders.

The father couldn't hear what the coach was saying but he didn't like him putting his arm around the boy, for one thing, and for another, the father didn't want the coach to be criticizing his son for not hitting those throws.

"Hey, that's my boy," he shouted at the coach, "let 'im be!" The coach and the boy looked where the father was sitting on the bleachers, his right shoulder thrust forward. The coach said something else to the boy that the father couldn't hear and the boy nodded. The coach raised his hand to the father in a friendly gesture and then walked back to the mound. The boy took a couple of practice swings from his new stance.

The coach threw ten more pitches. The boy missed the first four and then hit six in a row. As the father watched his son hit pitch after pitch, he was filled with a strange feeling in his throat and chest. He had never felt anything like it before. When the boy hit the last pitch high and far beyond the grassless patch of the diamond, the father wasn't aware until the ball hit the ground that he had leaped to his feet to watch it soar.

When the team ran out for fielding practice, the father saw that all the boys were wearing mitts except his son. The boy ran past the coach, and the coach again said something to him. The boy stopped and shook his head. The coach pointed to the outfield and the boy ran out to join several other boys.

A second man who had been sitting on the bench began hitting fly balls to the boys. He would call a boy's name and then hit a fly ball. The player called would try to catch it. The man called the boy's name. He tried to catch the ball, but it bounced off his bare hands and rolled away. When the ball hit the boy's hands, the father felt in the pit of his stomach a shock that radiated to his groin. He saw the boy shake his hands from the sting. The father looked at his own hands, surprised that they too were stinging.

After a few fly balls to other players, the man called the boy's name again. The boy ran several steps and this time he caught the ball after bobbling it slightly. Again the father felt the radiating shock but he also felt that same strange feeling as before rise in his chest and throat.

After the practice was over, the boy joined his father beside the bleachers. They walked down the hill through the park in silence. At one point the father tried putting his arm around the boy's shoulders but he was not accustomed to touching his son and took his arm away almost immediately. The boy did not know how to respond and did not acknowledge the gesture at all. When they reached home, the boy stopped at the bottom step and looked up at his father mounting to the porch.

"I didn't think about you needing a mitt," his father said, over his shoulder.

"I don't care about a mitt, Dad. Can I play or not?"

"Course you can play. Who said you couldn't?"

At that moment the man made a secret resolve to get his son a baseball mitt. He wanted to get him a new one until he saw the prices at the Western Auto store. He then turned to prowling through junk shops until he came across a second-hand mitt. The old lady who ran the shop wanted a dollar for it but he talked her down to fifty cents.

It was a mitt of the old style and was not formed into the shape of a scoop like the newer mitts he had seen at Western Auto. It lay out flat like a starfish and the fingers were not laced together at the ends. The webbing between the thumb and forefinger consisted of four badly rotted leather thongs. The mitt was so scuffed and dry and stiff it seemed the leather would crack and break if he tried to bend it.

The father hid the mitt in the shop and worked on it after the boy was in bed. He used motor oil to soften and clean the mitt, as he did his boots, until the leather was flexible and a rich dark brown. Looking at a picture of a mitt in an old Sears catalog, he repaired the webbing as best he could with doubled strands of baling twine.

The man finished the glove the night before the last game of the season. The boy would be starting the game in right field, and the father planned to get to the game early and surprise him with the mitt. He did not tell his wife about the glove. He wanted it to be a special thing between a man and his boy.

But he was delayed, and now he was hurrying up the path to the ball field, his right shoulder thrust far forward, the baseball mitt in a paper sack under his arm. The lights were on and the game had already started. The man could hear the high-pitched voices of the players calling encouragement to the pitcher or to the batter. He could hear the ball slapping into their leather mitts.

The man was angry that he was late, angry that replacing the needle bearings in the cylinder of a combine had taken so long, angry that he would be unable to surprise his son with the mitt before the game. He was angry too that his own stubbornness had prevented him from telling his wife about the glove and sending it to the ball field with her.

When the father reached the ball field, he saw that his son's team was at bat. He walked up to the fence on the first-base side. His son's team was in the third-base dugout. He saw his wife standing at the fence behind the team bench. She looked different and then he realized her hair was shining from recent washing and she didn't have her apron on. It struck him for the first time in years that she was pretty.

He searched the bench for his son. All the boys looked alike in the black caps with a yellow "L" and the black and yellow shirts with "LIONS CLUB" across the front. When the father finally picked out his son on the far end of the bench, he waved the paper sack above his head and motioned for the boy to come to him.

The boy had seen his father as soon as he appeared over the crest of the hill, but he sat quietly and made no sign. When his father waved the paper sack, however, the boy waved back but shook his head and held his palms up in front of him.

The father understood his son to mean not while the

team was batting, but he was not happy that he had gone to all this trouble with the mitt and now his son was waving him off. He started to pass through the gate in the first-base fence, but he stopped when his son stood up and shook his head and mouthed no.

Just then the batter hit a slow grounder to the second baseman who threw the ball to first base for the last out. When the father saw the boys on his son's team jump off the bench to take their positions in the field, he ran to the center of the diamond to intercept his son.

The son kept motioning to the father not to come onto the field all the while the father was pulling the mitt from the sack and thrusting it toward the boy. They met on the second-base side of the mound. The boy's face lit up when he realized it was a baseball mitt his father was holding out to him. He took it and for a moment just looked at it. Then he tried to fit it on his right hand. His face fell. The thumb and webbing were on the wrong side.

"Dad, it don't fit me."

"What you mean it don't fit? I bought and fixed it for you."

The boy's chin began to tremble. The father saw that he was going to cry. "It's made for a right-handed kid, Dad. You know I'm left-handed."

The father snatched the mitt from the boy. He was trembling, too, now. His face strained tight around his mouth and eyes.

"A mitt is a mitt!" he shouted. "Yours is good as any of those goddamn rich little bastards!" He swung the mitt in a wide arc to indicate the other players. "Don't tell me left-handed! Use the goddamn mitt!"

For an instant the whole scene seemed to center on the mitt as it completed its wide arc in the father's hand and then, almost by accident or coincidence it seemed, struck the boy across the face.

Then the father's rage was released and he couldn't seem to stop hitting the boy with the mitt. The boy cried out and cowered and the father hit him and hit him until, his arm poised again to strike, he looked around at the people in the bleachers and along the fences and behind the backstop.

Most sat or stood with their eyes turned away though some looked on. The mother was on her knees behind the dugout, her face buried in her hands. No one moved or made a sound except the coach who ran a few steps toward them but slowed when the man stopped hitting the boy. When the coach reached them, he held out his hand. The man lowered his arm without a word and the coach took the mitt. The coach helped the sobbing boy up and led him off the field. He put an arm around the boy's shoulders. The whole thing lasted perhaps thirty seconds.

The man stood behind the pitcher's mound and watched them go. When they reached the third baseline, he raised his hands as if to appeal to the crowd.

"I didn't know they made them for different hands," he said.

Then he thrust his shoulder forward and shouted at the coach's back, "Hey, where you think you're taking my boy?"

The boy turned and looked at the man like a stranger.

Vespers

Ascetic and slim in sabbath attire,
mantis comes to my window to prey.

His figure and piety all must admire
as he kneels on the sill of my window to prey.

Gnats and lacewings and midges attend;
cicadas and katydids strike up the choir,

and galilee moth and golgotha moth,
and angel-wing moth and crucifix miller

mutter and splutter and flutter
like candle flames, window glass bright

as an altar cloth. Abject and penitent,
rising from prayer, mantis embraces

the congregation, body and blood
for a pious old killer.

Evening Callers

Just at dusk three barred owls
whisper into the backyard elms.
For thirty minutes they circle
and swoop, or sit in silhouette
on dead branches high
against the fading light
and rollick a cacophony
of coughs and barks and howls
while a flurry of squirrels
chattering dire warnings
skitter for safety
on the undersides of limbs.

The Lap of Lechery

This is something I had forgotten. I remembered it about a year ago when I was cleaning some boxes out of my dad's garage after he died, and I came across an old yellow shirt of mine with blood on the front that brought it all back suddenly after almost thirty years. Since then I've been trying to figure out a way to go on from here.

It started when we got a new junior high coach after our seventh grade year. The first time any of us saw him he was leaning on a blocking dummy at one of the high school team's two-a-day practices. He was tall and freckled and lanky, and the sun lit up his red hair. The coach we'd had our seventh grade year had taken a high school job and moved away. We felt lost all summer. Losing a coach was almost like losing a parent. And getting a new coach was like trying out a new father. We wanted to like him but were afraid we wouldn't, or that he wouldn't like us, or even worse, that we wouldn't win with him.

But we shouldn't have worried. The first day of practice gave us an idea of what was in store. He wasn't a plodder like our old coach. He was young, bold, flashy, and casual. Our old coach had drilled us on boring fundamentals and stuck religiously to the straight T-formation. But our new coach taught a shifting combination of formations—single wing, double wing, split T, wing T, short punt—with exciting plays like double reverses, hook and ladder, double pitch out, hidden ball plays, and a secret weapon he called the Hope to God Pass. Our opponents never figured out what hit them. We razzled and dazzled them and by the time they came up with a defense that could slow us down, the game was out of reach.

A lot of times in practice, Coach would toss off his cap and get into the scrimmage himself. He was faster than any of us and could rifle a pass so hard that even our best end, Freddie Campo, couldn't handle it. I can still remember the way his tan shoes would reflect the light when he dropped back to pass or moved along behind the line on an option or a hand-off.

It didn't take us very long to develop a pretty intense hero worship. And Coach seemed to like having his crowd of admirers around him. We started hanging around after practice to listen to him talk. He would tell us stories about himself, and some dirty jokes. He talked to us like equals, the first adult who ever had.

After a while, we started going over to his house on Saturday mornings. We'd fight over who got to mow the lawn or help him haul trash to the dump. He had three kids, a girl and two little boys he was always dressing up in football jerseys and helmets. To make points, we even played touch football with them, though that was a bit of a strain.

His wife was as exciting and casual as he was. She was thin, pretty, dark-haired, and had a way of talking to you so intently you were sure you were the only male in the world and she was in love with you. Occasionally when she wasn't around, Coach complained good-naturedly to us that he didn't know how he ever got hooked into marrying a woman with such little tits. We laughed and tried to be as casual as he was, but we weren't very convincing. Dirty jokes were one thing, but when you started talking about a real woman, sex was harder to joke about for thirteen-year-olds.

The group that hung around the coach all the time were the seven best players on the team. We seven got favored treatment on the field, in the bus on the way to games, and even in his biology classes. We sat near the front, answered all the questions, and always got to help with the lab equipment and experiments. Being in that select group made us the envy of every other boy in the seventh and eighth grades.

So I guess that was why he only invited the gang to his house for the celebration after we finished the season undefeated. When we got there, he was drinking a beer, obviously not his first. This was something new for all of us. We lived in a conservative little Kansas town. On that Saturday evening all seven of us saw the first drunken man up close we had ever seen. When his wife ushered us into the family room, he began dancing, singing, slurring his words a little and sloshing beer onto the tile floor. His wife rolled her eyes at us in a humorous way and told him to control himself or we would tell our mammas. We all laughed and understood we weren't supposed to tell. And he did calm down, though we got a little uncomfortable when he kept trying to get us to drink a little beer, just to celebrate. None of us had ever done more than smell beer, and that at quite a distance.

But it was a good party. We went back over the whole

season and Coach had us laughing over the way we had made fools of the teams we had beaten with his fancy offense. We gloated over injuries we had caused or infractions we had gotten away with. Every time one of us told something about the season, Coach would tell a story about his college playing days and have us all awed and splitting with laughter at the same time. Then he started telling dirty jokes, raunchier than usual, and then he told us about a practical joke his fraternity brothers had played on him.

He said they found out when he was a freshman that he was a virgin, so they lined him up a blind date with a girl he didn't know was a notorious whore. He said they paid her $25 to get him to a particular parking spot by the lake so they could set up an ambush. She wore a full-length tan coat, he said, and they no sooner got to the parking place than she took it off and had nothing on underneath. He was so stunned, he said, that she got his fly open and grabbed his rod before he knew what was happening.

By this point in the story, we had gotten quiet. This wasn't just a dirty joke. It was a real story about real people about to have sex. It was the first time any of us had ever heard an adult talk about real sex.

His wife was sitting in an over-stuffed chair by the bar. Suddenly she said, "Matt, do you think you ought to be telling the boys this story?"

He seemed rattled and irritated for a second and got real red in the face, and then he gave her this nasty look we had all learned to fear in practice when he would turn it on someone who had screwed up a play. He looked at us and kind of snickered. "That's just what we need. A goddamned split-tail doing some arm-chair quarterbacking." Then he looked back at her. "I don't know why I ever married a woman with such little tits."

It was a reflex. We couldn't help it. We laughed, thinking it was a joke between them.

She didn't look at us. Her face was pale but blank. "Why did you marry me, Matt?"

"At the time you seemed like a good fuck. Besides, you got pregnant, remember?"

We kept trying to smile, still not sure this wasn't just another joke.

His wife sat still for a second or two and then got up and walked slowly out of the room. She said "Good-bye, boys" as she went through the door.

"Don't pay any attention to her," he laughed. "She's so damned sensitive about the size of her tits sometimes she loses her sense of humor about it."

We laughed again. This was the Coach, back in control, sharp, funny, casual. Still, the evening had lost its momentum. After Coach finished his story, we went home.

Basketball season started on Monday, and Coach had already tantalized us with his big plans for the team. Turnout for the first practice was disappointing, though. Only thirteen players showed up. To make it worse, two of the main seven weren't there. One had cracked a bone in his foot over the weekend and came to practice wearing a walking cast. The other kid just didn't show up. The next day he said his parents had decided sports were taking up too much of his time. As it turned out, we didn't miss him very much anyway. Like Coach said, he was always the wimpy one of the group.

Basketball season was like football season, except we didn't go undefeated. We had a wide-open offense, lots of run-and-shoot, and a fastbreak that flat ran our opponents off the court. Practices, after we learned the basic patterns, were mainly scrimmages. Coach would get into the action as much as possible. He had one heck of an accurate set shot from anywhere between twenty and thirty feet. He always played in his street clothes and the change would jingle in his pockets when he brought the ball down the court. Usually he'd pull up about twenty-five feet out and pop a one-handed set shot at the basket. If he swished it, he would wet two fingers in his mouth and hold them up. If he missed, he was always there for the rebound, elbows flying, and then he'd drive for a lay-up. He sure hated to miss a shot, and he hated to lose. So we were lucky, I guess, that we only lost one of our regular season games.

After that game, he called a practice right after the bus got back, ten o'clock at night. He ran us until midnight, shouting at us, driving us, ridiculing us when we made a bad play or looked tired. I think he might have kept us there all night except finally the school principal came into the gym and told him our parents were waiting to take us home. You had to admire somebody that wanted to win that bad. Most of us felt guilty we weren't as dedicated.

I don't know quite what happened in the championship game of the league tournament. We were playing a team we had beaten twice before. At the half we were fifteen points ahead. But then we turned cold and nothing seemed to work. We ran our fastbreak in slow motion. It was a little eerie, like the same thing had gone out of us all at exactly the same moment. Coach was fuming up and down the sideline, yelling and swearing at us. Finally he yanked the whole first team. I think he was mostly frustrated because he couldn't get in there and win it himself.

We lost by one point at the buzzer. He didn't even come into the locker room after the game. We found out later he had walked straight out of the gym, gotten into his car, and driven off. He didn't speak to us for days. Even in biology class he acted like we weren't there. Believe me, we were pretty demoralized. We felt like we had let him down.

We thought maybe things would get better when baseball season started. But something unexpected happened. Only eight boys signed the baseball roster on the locker-room bulletin board and only six showed up for practice the first day. Coach set us to playing catch and taking some batting practice and went back into his office. When he hadn't come out after an hour and a half, Freddie Campo and I told the others to knock off for the day. We gathered the equipment and took it into Coach's office. He was sitting at a table writing something on a piece of paper.

I said, "Coach, maybe Freddie and I can round up some guys for the team. I know there are others who want to play. Maybe they just missed the notice."

Freddie said, "I know three guys who played last year that had a penalty hour today for not doing their English homework. I think we can get some more guys. We gotta have a baseball team."

Coach looked at us for a minute and didn't say anything. His eyes had a strained look. "You guys are sticking with me, aren't you."

"Sure, Coach. We want to play baseball."

"OK, then, you two recruit some players. We'll put a winning team on the diamond yet."

And we tried, too. We called everybody or went to see them. We managed to get two guys, but no more. Nobody wanted to play baseball. They had either decided to lay out of sports for a while or to go out for one of the other spring teams—track, or golf, or some of those wimpy games. Freddie and I were pretty dejected when we went to Tuesday's practice. We felt like we had let Coach down just when he had shown some faith in us again.

The school principal was there but Coach wasn't. He announced that the school wouldn't be sponsoring a baseball team that spring, and that Coach would be assigned to other school duties, but he was sure if any of us wanted to try out for another team, we could still find a place. We could hardly believe it. For the first time ever, the school didn't have a baseball team.

That evening, Freddie and I went around to Coach's house. It was quiet there since his wife and kids had gone to stay with her mother. Coach was sitting in the kitchen eating a cold can of pork-n-beans and drinking a beer. There were a lot of empty food cans sitting around on the counter and the garbage was in several bags by the stove. We had been afraid Coach wouldn't be very glad to see us but he seemed ok.

We told dirty jokes for a while but our hearts weren't in it. Then Coach invited us to have a beer. "Season's over, boys. You're not in training." Neither of us had ever even tasted beer. I couldn't stand the smell of it myself. But we couldn't let him know that so we let him open a can for each of us and then we sat there and held them while he told jokes. "You're not drinking," he said after a while. "You guys need to cheer up. Missing one baseball season's not the end of the world. Come on, let's toast to your summer jobs."

Freddie and I both tried a sip of beer just as he said jobs. I coughed and Freddie choked. "What jobs?"

"My god, you guys act like you never had a drink of beer before. I want you to help me this summer. I have a deal with this truck farmer down near Wellington to deliver his produce. I rent a truck, hire a couple of helpers like yourselves, and haul vegetables all over south Kansas. That's how I make summer money when I'm not coaching. I'll pay you a buck and a half an hour. You pay for your own room and food. You can make a lot of money at this job. We never work less than a ten-hour day and we work seven days a week. That's over a hundred dollars a week all summer. You can't make that much bucking bales around here."

Neither of us had ever had a full-time job before. We were so excited we forgot all about baseball season. "We'll have to ask our folks."

"Sure, ask your folks. Tell them you'll be down there with me all summer. I'll keep an eye on you." Then he winked. "Who knows what kind of excitement we might get into down there. Did I ever tell you about the time I picked up a woman hitch-hiker in Missouri?"

It seemed almost too good to be true. A chance to earn good summer money and spend two months with Coach. We didn't have much trouble getting permission. Freddie's folks never had given him much supervision and mine liked the idea of the money. So in the middle of June we packed up our suitcases and rode out of town in Coach's big red Dodge.

The work was hard and steady at first. We'd load the truck Coach had leased, then we'd take turns going with him on deliveries, which were usually at night to keep the vegetables fresh. Coach told us story after story about his sex life, first with what seemed to us like hundreds of girls at college and then with his wife. We were eager listeners, but a little uncomfortable, too. This was real stuff, but it didn't seem quite right that he talked about his wife.

After a week, we hit a wet spell and couldn't work. Coach would loaf around the farm part of the day just in case the weather changed, then he'd say, "I'm horny. You boys want to go with me and get a piece of ass?" Of course, we never did. Then he'd go into town and not come back until early in the morning.

Our money began running low. On the fifth straight day of rain, Freddie caught the bus for home. He tried to talk me into going with him. "It's like before," he said. "He filled us full of big talk, and when it didn't work out, he went off and left us." He was right, I guess, and I'm not sure why I didn't go. Maybe I just wanted Coach all to myself for a while. Maybe I thought he would need me now that I was the only one of his gang left. When Coach found out Freddie was gone, he just shrugged. "I always thought Freddie was an asshole, anyway," was all he said.

Two days later it stopped raining, and the next day we were back at work. That night we took a delivery to Hutchinson. We had some problems unloading and so it was one in the morning before we got back on the road. I was so tired I felt drunk.

"Are we going all the way back to Wellington tonight?"

"No. I called Wichita at ten and got us a free place to sleep. We'll get up early and be back to the farm in time to get another load."

I slept the hour to Wichita, and only woke up when we stopped in front of a big white house with one light shining through the glass in the front door. I was standing there on the porch half asleep when a young woman in a bathrobe opened the door for us.

"Come in, Matt. Mother and Em took the children and went to Aunt Ellen's in Derby after you called. They had been planning to go in the morning anyway. She still doesn't want to see you. I stayed only because I have to go to work in the morning. Hello, young man," she said, turning to me, "I'm Anna. I'm Matt's sister-in-law. Matt, you two can use the twin beds in the spare room. The sheets are fresh. You know your way around. Good night." She went down the hallway and disappeared through a door and closed it after her.

"Bathroom's down the hall next to her room, if you need to go. Then come on upstairs, second door on the left. Did you notice that gorgeous set of tits on Anna? When the tits were passed out in this family, she got 'em all. Three other sisters including my wife and they're all flat-chested."

I snickered, but frankly I hadn't noticed anything. I was too sleepy. Coach went on upstairs.

I didn't even remember undressing and getting into bed when something woke me up and I realized I had been asleep. Coach was sitting up on the side of his bed. It was just starting to get light. I knew it was time to get up but I just couldn't move quite yet. I lay there with my eyes closed while he looked at me a long time, over a minute. Finally, he reached over and took his pants off the bedpost and slipped into them. When he stood up and went out of the room, I knew I had to get up, too. I put on my pants and shirt, picked up my shoes, and followed him.

When I got downstairs, I didn't see Coach but I thought I heard a noise in the kitchen so I went on down the hall toward the bathroom. Anna's door was partly open and there was just enough light to see the wall opposite the door. I cast my eyes down so as to get into the bathroom without looking into her room, when I suddenly heard Anna say something in a thick, sleepy voice. I thought she was calling to me, and an electric shock went through me. I looked timidly through the open doorway.

What I saw paralyzed me for a second. Coach was on top of Anna and she was struggling with him but like she was still half asleep and didn't quite realize what was going on. He pinned her wrists down and forced her knees apart with his knee and almost before I could swallow hard, he was screwing her. Anna quit struggling then and just lay there making a noise that sounded like crying.

I think at one time I knew what happened next, but now I've somehow gotten what actually happened confused with what I was afraid would happen or maybe with what I wish had happened until I can't tell them apart anymore.

At times I seem to have a vivid memory of watching Coach screwing Anna and her lying there and me standing against the dark wall by the door with this hot, breathless feeling in my chest, getting a hard-on. Coach finally grunts and rolls off her and goes past me out the door like he doesn't see me. I see a chance for my first piece of ass and pull off my pants. Anna keeps lying there with her eyes closed and her face turned away, except right when I try to climb on, she gives me a fierce look and starts hitting at my face with her fists. I run into the bathroom and close the door and sit down shaking on the floor. I notice my nose is bleeding. What seems like a long time after, I hear Coach calling my name. I get up and go out, afraid of what I'll have to face, but not knowing what else I can do. I find Coach and Anna quietly having breakfast as if nothing has happened. They want to know where I've been. Anna says you hurt yourself and cleans the blood off my face with a wet cloth. There's a place set for me and I sit down.

Just as vivid, though, is another recollection I have of feeling a sudden surge of burning shame rush through me when I see Coach forcing himself on Anna and her going limp underneath him. I turn away quickly and go into the bathroom and close the door and sit down shaking on the floor. As happens a lot when I get real excited or upset, my nose starts bleeding. What seems like a long time after, I hear Coach calling my name. Finally I get up and go out, not knowing how I'll face either one of them. I find Coach and Anna quietly having breakfast as if nothing has happened. They want to know where I've been. Anna says you hurt yourself and cleans the blood off my face with a wet cloth. There's a place set for me and I sit down.

The third way I remember it is just as real. At first I'm sort of paralyzed by what I see, but when I hear Anna whimpering, hot anger rushes into my throat and I hit Coach in the side with a running shoulder block that carries both of us clear across the bed and into the wall. When we roll, I end up under him and quick as a rattlesnake he knees me in the nuts and starts hitting me in the face. I black out and the next thing I know I'm sitting on the bathroom floor shaking and my nose is bleeding. What seems like a long time after, I hear Coach calling my name and I get up and go out, even though I'm scared to death of what he will do to me. I find Anna and Coach quietly having breakfast as if nothing has happened. They want to know where I've been. Anna says you hurt yourself and cleans the blood off my face with a wet cloth. There's a place set for me and I sit down.

After breakfast, Anna said good-bye to us. She gave Coach a kiss on the cheek, and even gave me a hug with one arm around my shoulders. Coach and I got in the truck and drove back to Wellington. I walked through the rest of that day, and the rest of the summer, in a daze. I worked until the middle of August when the vegetable season was over, and then I went home on the bus and only found out when school started that Coach had taken a job selling insurance in Omaha and wouldn't be back. I never saw him again. I don't think I actually forgot about that summer. It was more like I just quit thinking about it.

Now I'm so mixed up about it I almost start thinking I made up the whole thing or that it was a bad dream. But then I get out the bloody shirt I found in the box and I know the story is true. It really happened to me. For some reason, though, I just can't figure out what happened in that bedroom. I'm sure of only one thing. Whatever happened made all the difference in the way my life turned out. Now, if I could just figure out what it was.

Premonition

You were reading the Sunday paper
and I was so engrossed in a book
and the warmth of our Boston Terrier
snugged up tight against my thigh
that I did not notice you had put
the paper down and slipped away
until I looked up and saw the wrinkles
relaxing on your palm tree pillow
and the lamp light pooling
on your empty chair. Except
for the hollow echo of the furnace
the house was quiet. Outside
the almost transparent shadow
of a bird was moving away
across the frozen grass.

The Notice

One by one that summer the farmer watched his heifers die of the heat. He and his wife of forty years worked hard to bring the last one through. But just when they thought they had succeeded, it developed on its eye an ulcerated tumor. Now he would have to kill it, put it out of its misery. He called the neighbor to come with his pickup to haul away the carcass. Then he hitched his coverall straps over his workshirt, lifted his Co-op cap from the peg, and picked up his rifle from the kitchen corner.

He drove the tractor with the front-loader across the pasture until he came upon the heifer standing belly-deep in dusty pigweed. The animal was backed into a fence corner with its head down as if to shield its raw and dripping eye from the sun. He took a hollow-point from the bib pocket of his overalls and looked for a moment at the way the sun glinted off the copper casing. He shrugged and slipped the load into the chamber and lifted the rifle to his shoulder, but instead of shooting, he stumbled forward half a step and dropped the rifle in the weeds. His hands went to his mouth and he retched as if to vomit. Then he took a running step and embraced the cow's head and bit deep into the growth with his teeth.

The heifer bawled and backed and swung its head, trying to shake him off. But he hung on and tore out ravenous bites and chewed and swallowed until he had eaten the side of the heifer's face clean of hide and hair and eye and cancer.

He let go then and fell on his back in the weeds. His face and arms and upper body were covered with gore. The animal ran wildly about at first but gradually slowed to a walk. It circled back and stood staring down at him with its one remaining eye.

That's when the neighbor drove into the pasture.

That afternoon, the farmer found himself sitting on a milking stool in the barn. This was where the neighbor left him before stopping briefly at the house and then going on. The farmer realized he was waiting in the urine-rank gloom to sicken and die. Occasionally, a wave of nausea would come. But it would pass. Just before dark his wife came and stood in the barn door looking at him. Then she went away without saying a word. He heard her back their rusty old Chevy out of the shed and drive up the lane to the county road and turn toward town. Then, it seemed as if he blinked and it was morning. He had slept sitting on the milking stool all night.

The heifer was bawling from the lot. He walked out into the light and saw that the wound on the animal's face was covered now with a scab. He broke a bale of alfalfa into the feed trough. The heifer lowered its muzzle to the hay and ate steadily, looking at him warily with its solitary eye. He stripped off his bloody clothes, engaged the gears of the windmill, and slid under the spout of icy water. After he had scrubbed himself, he left his things where they had fallen and walked naked to the house. On the kitchen table he found his wife's note. She would be at her sister's a few days until she could decide what to do. He paused dripping over the note, then dressed in a fresh shirt and overalls and sat on the porch watching the heifer graze in the pasture. That was Wednesday.

The old farmer did nothing the next eight days but feed the heifer, scrub under the windmill spout, and sit on the porch in a fresh shirt and clean overalls. The heifer ate well every day and began to put on flesh. The scab was clean and healing. On the ninth day he saw that the scab was gone and where the cancerous eye had been was a perfectly healed pink-skinned scar the size and shape of a baby's hand. He got the hay truck started and drove to town. He went first to the newspaper office and placed an ad, and then he walked up and down the sidewalks and into the drugstore and the grocery. He noticed that people were keeping a little distance so he knew that the neighbor had talked, or perhaps his wife or her sister. Likely, after the notice came out, his wife would not come back. But that was all right, everything was going to be all right now.

The notice appeared in the Services Offered section of the classifieds in the next edition of the paper. "Cancer Eater Will Eat Your Livestock Cancers for Cash or Barter. Cure Guaranteed Or You Don't Pay," and then it gave his telephone number.

He was sitting on his porch when he read the notice. Now all he had to do was wait for the phone to ring.

All This Moving Apart

It's easy to see why some find it
hard to believe. The cosmos
compressed into a cube

that could rest easily in a teaspoon.
And then the rupture,
the chaos, the unimaginable violence

spattering across even more
unimaginable distances,
galaxies and other wonders

racing away from each other
with ever increasing velocity.
But there it is.

Mathematical calculations,
says the scientist, and the latest
astrophysical observations

lead to conclusions inescapable.
It must be true. But those
who watch white crowned sparrows

feeding along the fence row
and feel the frost under their feet
as they walk the winter field

are obliged to ask the question:
How could this unimaginable
sequence of impossible events

lead at last to us?
The wind tumbles a crow
into the upper limbs of a dead elm

that has shed great sleeves
of bark to shatter on the ground.
Our hands find each other

as the crow's clawed feet find
a branch thirty feet above.
It is too improbable. The mind

cannot encompass the paradox
that reaches across the vast wastes
and deserts of cosmic time

to the crow's black claws
grasping the dead branch,
to my hand pressing into yours,

to the heat we exchange
clinging together in all
this cosmic moving apart.

Keeping In In and Out Out

True red resides
not in the robin's breast
but in the cardinal
in the snowy spruce
keeping counsel
behind his black mask.

This window,
a frame through which
to contemplate
the winterscape?
Or a barrier
keeping in in
and out out?

Mallards like crumpled rags
cluttering the frozen pond
beyond the fence are waiting
for spring's dark spiders
to rise up through the ice.

The wind has bleached
all color from the sky.

Every needle of the spruce
stands out.

A Parable of Plumbing

It was 5:37 Friday afternoon and Gerald Whitley was waiting for a plumber. He was late and Gerald was growing impatient.

On the previous Wednesday morning Gerald had looked at the stack of accounts in his in-basket and realized that every No. 2 Wallace Invader in his tooled leather pencil holder was dull. Suddenly the rest of Gerald's life seemed to him unbearably long.

Gerald had wanted to be an accountant even before he was left to fend for himself by the deaths of his parents when he was sixteen. He trained single-mindedly for the profession in college. Every day of his seventeen years with Fairbanks, Barker, and Dean, Inc., he went to work eager to unravel the tangles of inventory valuations, bank assets, and tax returns. Each afternoon he took home with him a briefcase full of accounts to while away the evening. He left himself little opportunity for a personal life and in fact seemed to need little. He did have a woman friend, Sally, a reference librarian with whom he went out occasionally for a movie or a meal. They had been "dating" for five years. They had never been intimate. For Gerald, accounting seemed to be all he needed of work and recreation, comfort and sympathy.

On that Wednesday afternoon in his thirty-seventh year, Gerald walked about under the chapel-like arch of two old sycamores in his backyard instead of digging into his briefcase for a little work before dinner. It was then the idea popped into his head.

He would convert his garage into an apartment. He examined the idea and decided after careful analysis that this was just the thing he needed to do, for four very good reasons:

1. He would be able to busy his hands with the actual rebuilding. Carpentry. He remembered helping his father with simple projects. He could handle a hammer, he was sure. And wiring. Electricity he understood. It was logical. His father had told him, "Just keep your nuts tight," an aphorism his father thought both wise and witty and for which Gerald had long since forgiven him.

2. Sally could recommend do-it-yourself books that would guide him.

3. He would be converting a portion of his domicile into an income-producing property.

4. He would be creating a tax write-off. Depreciation of income-producing property was deductible.

He was greatly relieved. The garage apartment idea made him feel almost like himself again.

Gerald had not gone far with his planning, however, when it occurred to him that an apartment would need plumbing. He knew nothing about plumbing. He would have to hire a plumber to do the work, and that would cost money he hadn't planned on.

He let out discrete inquiries in plumbing circles. He was seeking not the best plumber nor the fastest. He merely wanted a plumber competent to do the job at a reasonable fee. He was given the name of a plumber near retirement who charged less than younger, more ambitious plumbers.

Gerald made an appointment to meet the plumber at 5:10 Friday afternoon. He wasn't expecting much. Still, he wasn't prepared for what he got.

The plumber was late. Twenty-seven minutes late to be exact. Gerald prized promptness next only to accuracy with figures. Though Gerald generally abhorred sports metaphors, he had to admit that this was definitely strike one.

Strike two was the plumber's appearance. He pulled up in a rusted-out station wagon of uncertain make, year, and color. It looked as if it had been rescued from a salvage yard. Except for the driver's seat, the entire wagon was crammed with a filthy jumble of pipes, fittings, wrenches, crumpled fast-food bags, even a broken toilet. On the front bumper was a badly faded sticker,

Your SHIT is my BREAD & BUTTER!

In the back window another sticker read,

Plumbers lay STEEL PIPE!

The plumber wore threadbare grease-stained coveralls. His

greasy gray hair strung down to his shoulders from under an old black felt cowboy hat. He had a week of dirty beard stubble and the corners of his mouth were crusted with some unknown substance.

Gerald decided before the first word was spoken not to wait for strike three. He would take the first opportunity he found to send this old bumbler away as gently and as quickly as possible.

The old plumber's first question, however, threw Gerald off. "You wanta use copper, galvanized, or plastic?"

Gerald had assumed that pipes were—well, pipes. "D-does it matter?" he stammered. "I mean, it's a very small job," he said, trying to be discouraging.

"Well," the plumber said, "it don't matter to me. I just thought you knowed what you wanted." Again, Gerald felt himself at a disadvantage. He sought new ground.

"What would you recommend?"

"Copper's best all-round, but it's damn high." Cost. Now here was something Gerald knew about.

"A plumber of your calibre probably only works with the best material. But I, well, I need to cut as many corners as possible or my little project won't pay. So I guess I'd better——"

"Like I said," the plumber broke in, "it don't matter to me. Most small jobs I use plastic. It's cheaper than copper or galvanized and it don't scale up inside, though it will split if your line freezes. So you have to insulate good. CPVC is best for your supplies but you can get by with PVC for your wastes. PVC ain't code though so you'd hafta watch out for the city inspector."

This tangle of unfamiliar terminology dazed Gerald.

His mouth was open but no words came. The plumber was warming to the project now, though, and didn't seem to notice.

"You got a water line in the back I can tie in to?"

Gerald shrugged.

"Does your waste run to the front or does it come out the back towards the alley?"

"Waste?"

"Sewer," said the plumber.

"Oh," said Gerald. "I have no idea. Is it important?"

"Well, it is unless your renter is gonna use a slop-jar or a outhouse." Levity. Gerald should have guessed from the bumper stickers. He distrusted levity.

"I really don't know," said Gerald coldly.

"I spose I could go to City Hall and look through the records, but they'd want know why I'm lookin. You'd have to pay the city fee and the inspector would come out. Is that what you want?"

This made sense to Gerald. Why install cheap pipes and then spend the money you saved on city fees?

"Is there another way to find out?"

"I could try findin 'em myself."

"How would you do that?"

"The sewer's too deep for a metal detector," said the plumber. "Besides, it's clay. I'd have to witch for 'em."

Gerald couldn't help smiling now. Witching? Was this a practical joke? Gerald vaguely recalled water witching stories from grade school.

"You're not telling me, are you, that a plumber uses a forked stick to find water pipes?"

"If you're looking for ground water, you can use a

green peach wand. But we got galvanized pipe at least two feet down and a deep sewer line. Have you got any weldin rods?"

"Where would I get welding rods? I'm an accountant."

"Well, they're not as reliable, but I've had luck on occasion with wire hangers."

Gerald almost laughed out loud. This had to be a practical joke. Still, he was mildly curious and went into the house to retrieve some clothes hangers.

"The kind that ain't painted work better," the old plumber called after him.

The plumber cut and straightened two of the clothes hangers Gerald brought and bent each into an "L" shape. He held them in front of him like a pair of pistols and began pacing slowly across the yard. Gerald again almost laughed out loud at the ridiculous figure he made, like a dissolute old outlaw in a low-budget western movie.

When the "gun barrel" portions of the hangers rotated towards each other and crossed, the laugh died in Gerald's throat.

"Here's something," the plumber said. "It might be pipe." He moved up the yard toward the house and paced again. The wires crossed a second time. Gerald stared in disbelief.

"There it is again," the old plumber said and sighted back across the yard. "It could be the same pipe. It runs straight out from the house." Gerald's eyes were wide but his mouth was ready to sneer. Did the old man think he was so easily taken in?

"If the sewer line comes out the back, it should be just

about here," the old plumber said, indicating an area just south of the garage. The plumber paced again, and about three paces from the wall the wires rotated very slowly and crossed. The plumber backed up a step. Gerald pursed his lips when the wires reversed their rotation. The plumber moved a dozen feet closer to the house and paced again. Again the wires rotated slowly and then reversed when he backed up.

"That must be the sewer," said the plumber, "but it's deep. Did you see how slow them wires moved?"

"I saw," Gerald said, barely concealing his sarcasm. He had always prided himself on his scientific habit of mind and was not inclined to believe in such as this. "I suppose the wires where attracted by—what? Magnetism? Some kind of sympathetic resonance plumbers have with the water deities?"

The plumber looked puzzled. "Oh, you mean how does it work?"

"Okay," Gerald said. "How *does* it work?" thinking this must be the punch line.

"I don't know," said the plumber, apparently missing the irony in Gerald's voice or choosing to ignore it. "I just know it does—most of the time, anyway. My daddy was a plumber and he taught me how to do it. It's a right handy thing to know, I guess, if you're a plumber. I don't know what good it'd do anybody else." He laughed and switched back to the business at hand. "If you dig where them wires crossed, you should strike pipe and I can tie in there. Any idea when you want me to start?"

Gerald had had enough and decided to end this ridiculous charade. It was his own fault. He should have called one of the younger plumbers instead of wasting time on this senile imposter.

"Actually, I'm not sure when I'll start," Gerald said, turning toward the front where the plumber had parked. "I'll call you. I have your number, I think."

"Don't you want me to work up an estimate?" the plumber asked.

"No, no," Gerald said, "I think I've heard enough."

"Look," the plumber said, "if you don't want me to do the work, just say so. It won't be the first job I ever missed out on. But if you want me do it, don't wait too long. I'm plannin to retire here in a few months."

"Sure. I won't wait too long," Gerald said. The old plumber drove off in a cloud of oil smoke. Gerald went to the backyard and picked up the wires. Witching. He was embarrassed that he had given it even momentary credibility.

He sat down on the back step. The sun was sitting on the horizon. A robin was singing in the mulberry tree. Gerald felt his enthusiasm for the garage project ebb. The emptiness of Wednesday morning came over him again. Inexplicably, tears welled up in his eyes.

Gerald became aware of his hands. He looked down. The wires. It seemed to him that he had sensed something in them, a tingle perhaps, a vibration. He stood up. There it was again. Had he been squeezing them without realizing it? Were his hands falling asleep? He shook them to get the circulation going.

He held the wires out in front of him as the plumber had done. He felt silly and looked around to make sure no one could see him.

He stood against the garage and paced slowly across the yard. When he reached the spot where the plumber had said the sewer was buried, the wires slowly crossed in his hands like a greeting. Gerald tried it again in several places along the same line. Every time the wires rotated as if of their own volition. The tingle in his hands was more certain. A faint yet definite vibration.

Still his skepticism was strong. Was he deceiving himself? He went to an area in his sideyard where he couldn't be sure there were any pipes. He paced straight out from the side of his house until the wires rotated and crossed. Gerald stuck his pocket knife into the ground to mark the place and moved closer to the street. The wires rotated again. He marked this place with a chip of bark. Near the curb Gerald found the round metal cover of his city water meter hidden in the grass. When he stood on it and sighted toward the backyard, the wood chip and the pocket knife lined up almost perfectly. The moment was wonderful and disturbing. He was afraid to trust what he had just seen with his own eyes.

Gerald decided to call Sally. She tended to be skeptical and hard-headed and practical. If she confirmed what had happened, maybe he could begin to trust what he had experienced.

When Sally got there, he took her out under the sycamores and explained what he wanted her to do. He crossed the yard twice to demonstrate and then put the wires into her hands.

"Is this some kind of turn-on for kinky sex, Gerald? No? Well, a girl never gives up hope." She laughed. "Clothes hangers are a little out of my line, though. I'm a

simple log-chain and rubber apron kind of girl at heart."
She laughed again. Gerald frequently had to forgive Sally
for making coarse jokes. It was one of her weaknesses. He
tried not to be offended now by her failure to appreciate the
seriousness of the moment.

"I saw the wires move when the plumber held them
and then it happened to me," he explained again. "Go
ahead and walk across the yard. If they don't cross for you,
you can laugh all you want."

"You're so sexy when you're mystical," she mocked,
but set out across the yard anyway. When she reached the
place where the wires had rotated before, they turned in her
hands. As soon as the wires moved, she threw them down
and shook her hands in revulsion.

"What are you trying to do to me?" she cried. "Five
years I've waited for you and this is what I get for it?" She
was trembling now and her face was flushed. "Don't you
have any idea what a woman wants, Gerald? What I
want?"

Gerald   looked   at   her   with   surprise   and
incomprehension.

"What the hell? Play your stupid self-involved tricks
on someone else!" She ran to her car and drove away.

Gerald felt loneliness settle around him in the
fading late-afternoon light. This wasn't the reaction he had
expected. Why had she gotten so upset? Well, she would
calm down.

Gerald looked across the backyard under the empty
arch of the sycamores. He was still craving validation.
Sally's reaction had been anything but conclusive.

Gerald lay awake most of the night. Recurring images

in his mind of bent clothes hangers rotating rotating rotating and of pipes lying secret underground projecting invisible lines of force in every direction kept him too agitated to sleep.

Finally, it dawned on him that the whole thing might have a scientific explanation. Yes, that was it. If he could get an explanation, from an actual scientist, then everything could be set in order again. He found some peace then and slept.

All through the long week end Gerald busied himself with work brought home from the office. In the late afternoon hours he found himself needing to talk to Sally. But each time he called, her machine answered. She did not return his calls.

First thing Monday morning, Gerald called the Physics Department at the local college. He asked for the department head.

"You may think I'm crazy, but I wouldn't call you about this if I hadn't seen it with my own eyes. A plumber came to my place Friday and located buried water pipes with clothes hangers. I was wondering if there's a scientific explanation for such a thing."

The line was quiet for a few seconds, but Gerald heard no laugh or a snicker coming through the hollow hum of the receiver.

"Can you tell me what he did with the hangers?"

Gerald described what had happened as precisely as he could. "And I tried it, too," he added, "and so did another person, and it worked the same for both of us." Gerald was surprised to hear himself trying to convince the physics professor rather than inquiring about the scientific explanation as he had planned.

"Would you mind if I came out and had a look?" asked the department head. "Right now I can't say that I know of any scientific reason for what you have described. Maybe if I see it for myself, I will have a better idea." They arranged to meet in Gerald's backyard that afternoon at two.

Gerald then called the old plumber to see if he could be there when the physics professor came.

"Why are you callin in a perfessor?" the plumber asked. "What does he know about plumbing?"

"It's not the plumbing. I want him to explain how the witching works."

"I showed you the pipes. What else you need to know?"

"It's just that it was, well, like magic. I thought if you were there, maybe you could show the professor, just in case. . . ."

"In case he don't believe it? Look, Mr., uh, Woodrow, I work for a livin. I don't have time to worry if some perfessor thinks I can find pipes. If I can't find 'em one way or another I'm out of business. Now I'm ready to do the job anytime you want me to. But if it ain't plumbing, I'm afraid it ain't my problem."

Just before lunch that day at work, Gerald made an excuse not to return to the office that afternoon, the first time in anyone's memory that he had been absent. Barker spoke for all the partners when he expressed his concern. Gerald lied. A stomach bug. He was certain he would be only temporarily indisposed. His real reason for leaving work was unsettling enough. The lie he told to cover it was vastly complicating. Gerald had a conscience like a balance sheet, and the lie troubled him like an unresolved shortage at the end of the business day.

When the physics professor arrived that afternoon, Gerald offered to demonstrate. The professor asked him not to.

"Just show me how to hold the wires and let me walk around on my own. That way I won't be influenced."

The professor held the wires like Gerald showed him and began to walk slowly about the yard. The wires wavered slightly to the professor's stride, but they never rotated and crossed. After ten minutes, he handed the wires to Gerald and asked him to try it.

Gerald walked in the places the wires had rotated before but this time they were dead in his hands. He went to a place in the sideyard where he had found the water main on his own. This time the wires crossed.

"See!" Gerald cried. "It works! They crossed right where I found the water main Friday afternoon!"

The professor took the wires from Gerald again. "Check to make sure I'm holding them correctly," he said. Then he walked where Gerald had walked. The wires did not move. Gerald took the wires back and retraced his steps. This time the wires were dead. Both men stood silently looking at the wires in Gerald's hands.

"I have to go back to the office," the professor said. He looked sympathetically at Gerald. "Maybe you stepped a certain way and the wires swung to your body motion. Maybe your hands just moved the slightest amount." His voice was not sarcastic.

"No," Gerald said. "The wires turned on their own.

And what about the other person? It happened to her, too."

"I don't know. Maybe you both stepped a certain way," the professor said again.

The professor left. Gerald sat on his back steps while the sun slipped down the afternoon. After a time, he took up the wires and paced about the backyard under the arch of the sycamores. The wires did not cross. The energy he had felt before did not return.

Finally, Gerald carried the bent hangers onto the back porch and laid them aside. He went into the kitchen and fixed his solitary dinner. Now and then he would look out the window above the sink. The backyard seemed an empty place.

All ideas of converting the garage to an apartment had faded. When his dinner was cooked, he ate in front of the television watching Wheel of Fortune. He did not try to call Sally. He read for a while and went to bed early.

At one in the morning he woke suddenly out of a troubled sleep gripped by a firm conviction. He dressed and went to the back porch and picked up the wires. Then he got his pick and shovel and for the rest of the night he dug trenches. He dug in the sideyard and backyard, everywhere the wires had rotated, two feet down. Where the plumber had witched for the sewer, he dug a deeper trench. When the sun came up, his lot looked like it had been trenched for combat, but in every trench Gerald had struck pipe.

At nine sharp that Tuesday morning, Gerald called the office to tell them he was taking the day off. He was still indisposed. This time the lie didn't bother him at all. It took him until afternoon to fill in the trenches and tamp down the dirt securely. Then he laid aside his pick and shovel and went straight to the library where he found Sally by the world atlases. He was completely covered with mud and looked like he had just been molded from clay and set in motion. Before she could protest or run for safety, he wrapped her in his arms and held her tightly while he whispered intently in her ear. He cried as he whispered and the muddy tears ran down his face and into her hair.

After they were married, Gerald and Sally built a new house in the suburbs. Gerald started his own accounting firm. They didn't convert Gerald's former domicile into rental property or sell it. Instead they tore down the old house and garage, which were little better than ruins anyway, and let the lot run to grass. There under the arch of the ancient sycamores they often came evenings or Sunday afternoons to walk or picnic with their two daughters who were the pride of those magic years.

Now and then, though, some householder in the older part of town would wake of a morning to find that a trench had mysteriously appeared in his yard during the night. In the bottom of the trench was water pipe every time.

Hummingbird

The hailstorm battering
the roof after midnight
roused us from our sleep
to watch the nickel-sized
bullets ricocheting
off the deck. In the morning
the gravel drive and lawn
were littered with leaves
the hail had cut from the maples
and oaks, and on my
front walk as I stepped out
for the morning paper lay
a ruby-throated hummingbird,
wings now still that alive
had been a blur, and
of a sudden, along with
the one hundred sixty-one
human lives lost
in the Joplin tornado,
I grieved to count the toll
of all the smaller souls.

Salt of the Earth

Head bent over a plate of steaming eggs and hash browns, Alfred was picking up the salt shaker when an unbidden thought made him pause. A country tune played in the background on the diner's juke box, "Third-rate romance, low-rent rendezvous. . . ."

Blisters. That was Alfred's unbidden thought. Broken blisters. The sting of salty sweat rubbed into broken blisters.

The buttery biscuit Alfred had just swallowed turned into a hot unstable ball in his gut. Lately it seemed that every time he got a good start on a meal, some nauseating thought would up and ruin it. He never believed getting old would be like this. His stomach oscillated on an uncertain axis and his hand trembled. He set down the shaker.

The waitress came to his booth to top off his coffee. She was heavy with a huge bosom. She smelled like sausage. When she leaned over the end of his table, he couldn't stop himself. Here came another one. He closed his eyes and imagined her naked.

He broke into a sweat. He couldn't get the picture out of his mind. Her and him naked together, her breasts like eggs sunny side up over huge mounds of hash browns, their ample bellies rubbing together like great syrupy pancakes. And all over both of them . . . blisters . . . like on sizzling links of sausage . . . blisters . . . that broke and stung with the salty friction of their lovemaking. The picture faded. He felt better.

He opened his eyes and plucked a purple daisy from the plastic bouquet on his table. "Hilda," he whispered, "you're still the sexiest thing on two wheels!" He thrust the flower toward her.

Hilda blushed. "Oh, Al, you're just too romantic!" she declared loud enough for everyone to hear. "Lookit this, ever body. Al give me a flower." She leaned down and whispered in his ear. "You just better watch out young man when I git home I'll turn you ever way but loose!" She clapped him on the back and they laughed till the tears came.

Then Hilda went off with her pot of coffee to tend the other customers and Alfred turned happily back to his plate. Maybe him and Hilda wasn't as young as they once was but by god she could still cure what ailed him.

He tapped a generous sprinkling of salt over his steaming eggs and taters. That coffee sure smelled good.

Robins Keep Their Secrets

Suppose for a moment
they do not migrate south
in winter as everyone assumes

but instead don black hoods
and abandon leaf strewn lawns
for the white freedom of December skies.

Were you to look just so
you might see flocks of them
flashing their fiery badges

in sunlight slanting just above
the tops of distant trees.
And were you walking in the woods,

where ice is just beginning
to skim the creek that's pooling
behind the fallen sycamores and oaks,

if you listened, you might hear them
scratching in the bracken,
and see their shadows mirrored

in the surface of the stream
as they bow to drink
at the swifter narrow sluices.

This Lie of Language

We turn and turn this garden dirt
and beneath every shovelful the same
expressionless face stares back.

An acorn high in the canopy
lets go and ricochets randomly
through the branches.
Does the oriole before it sings
form an intent that
when we hear its song we say
that bird plans to mate or eat
or explain what God
had in mind for all of this?

And thus we grieve
the distance we cannot cross
between this lie of language
and the truth of dirt and branch
and bird and bone.

The Red Stone Mystery

Preston Gault was looking for a screw driver he thought he might have left in the back of the bedroom closet. But when he opened the closet door, he was surprised to encounter a strange man with a friendly face.

Preston was in the process of finishing a building project he had started while taking his first academic leave after eighteen years as a college professor. On his leave application Preston had claimed that he wanted to get back in touch with his creative side. Poetry had always moved him. In first grade he had made a Mother's Day card. He had copied into it the most beautiful poem he knew at the time. "How now, brown cow, grazing in the green green grass." His mother laughed until tears ran down her face. She made Preston read it to her friends, and they all laughed, too.

In second grade he had written a play about a baseball player trying to find out who had broken his favorite bat. The teacher thought it was cute and made him and the other members of his class act it before the whole school. Everyone forgot their lines, even him.

In fifth grade he and a friend began writing a novel about the Indian wars. They, of course, were the heroes. They kept the manuscript of the novel hidden in their clubhouse. Preston's older brother and his friends raided the clubhouse. They used some of the pages of the novel to wipe with after taking a crap in the woods. They started a fire with the rest.

Through high school and college, Preston continued to consider himself a writer and scribbled ideas for poems and stories in a private notebook. But he never seemed to have time to develop his ideas into finished works. Someday, he told himself.

When Preston started his academic leave, his wife talked him into taking a few weeks at the beginning to add three rooms to their old house to make it more attractive for re-sale. After all, he had five whole months. He could have the rest of his leave time to write. Now the renovation project was not finished, his leave was almost over, and he was beginning feel the opportunity slipping away.

At first Preston thought the stranger with the friendly face was one of the workmen. The place was crawling with them, carpenters, electricians, plumbers. But this man called Preston by his childhood nickname, something no one had done in more than forty years.

"Hello, Buzzy." The man held out his hands, palms up. "I'm here to offer you a choice between these two things."

On one palm was a red stone about the size and shape of a peach pit. On the other was a metal tablet like a wall plate for a light switch.

Preston was suspicious. "How did you know my old nickname?"

"You have nothing to be afraid of, Buzzy." The man's friendly expression did not waver. He extended his hands invitingly. "Either choice is good."

Preston examined the objects more closely. "I choose one and it's mine, just like that?"

"Just like that."

"If I choose the red rock, what am I actually getting?"

"I can't tell you. But I can tell you about the golden tablet."

"*Golden* tablet?"

"Yes. Twenty-four caret gold."

"You're kidding," said Preston. "You're offering to hand me a good sized piece of twenty-four caret gold?"

"Yes."

"How much is it worth?"

"I can assure you, Buzzy, it's very valuable. See for yourself how heavy it has become."

Preston took the tablet in his hand and hefted it. It was as heavy as a brick but small enough to slip easily into his pocket.

"How much is the rock worth?" Preston turned to examine the red stone again, but it was no longer in the man's other hand.

"Don't worry about the red stone, Buzzy. I'll have it ready when you need it. Anyway, you've chosen the tablet. Use it well. The screwdriver you were looking for is on the floor behind you."

"Oh, yeah. Thanks." Preston turned to retrieve it. When he straightened up, the man was gone. Preston quickly slipped the golden plate into his pants pocket. He checked outside the closet door to make sure no one was in the bedroom. The clock on the dresser said 4:29.

Preston felt a sudden urgency. He went to the kitchen without taking time to change out of his work clothes. He hadn't shaved in several days. His wife was there.

"Where are you going looking like that?" she chided him.

"Hardware store," he lied. He didn't want her to know what he was up to.

"Are you forgetting you promised to go to the church with me? I need your help with my meeting."

"I'll come along later. The electricians will need these supplies first thing in the morning."

He hurried out. She yelled after him to clean himself up before he came to the church. He wasn't listening. He just had time, he thought, to get to a jewelry store before it closed.

As Preston drove through rush hour traffic, he could feel the weight of the metal plate in his pocket. He very much wanted it to be gold as the man had claimed it was. He could use the money.

When Preston opened the door of the jeweler's shop, the counter girl looked up and saw an unshaven man in dirty clothing entering the store. He was nervous and agitated and had his hand clinched in his pocket. She had heard on her car radio that morning about a rash of daylight robberies in the city. She turned pale and put her finger on the silent alarm button under the counter. It was connected directly to the police department.

Preston hurried to where she stood behind the glass-topped display case. "Let me see the jeweler," he demanded.

"I'm sorry," the girl said. "Mr. Abrams is busy right now." She didn't want to reveal that she was there alone.

"It will have to be you, then," Preston said, breathing

heavily. His voice was urgent and his expression wild. He looked at the front door nervously. "Let's go to the back of the store."

"That's against store policy," the young woman said in a trembling voice. She pushed the alarm button. Preston stepped around the display counter. He grabbed the girl by the arm and pulled her through the curtain that covered the door to the back room. He kept his other hand clinched in his pocket.

"I need to test something to see if it's gold," Preston said impatiently. "How do you do that?"

The girl was terrified. She had no idea what Preston was talking about. She looked around desperately and saw a small brown eye-dropper bottle. She had seen the jeweler put the fluid from it on rings and bracelets before he looked at them through his eye piece. It was nothing more than cleaning fluid, but she did not know this.

"Here! Use this!" She grabbed the bottle and thrust it at Preston. "Take it, but please don't hurt me." Her voice rose to a hysterical pitch and she began to cry.

Preston was stunned. He had not even noticed that she was upset. Why was she screaming? This was terrible. If anyone came, how would he explain about the tablet? Preston grabbed the small bottle and ran through the curtain into the front of the store.

What he encountered there stopped him in his tracks, two police officers pointing their guns at him. When he tried to throw his hands above his head, the officers fired.

Preston saw orange flowers bloom in slow motion from the barrels of the pistols like time-lapse photography. The bullets buzzed at him like black bees. How slowly they came! He was amazed at how easy it was to dodge them. He ducked behind the display case and scrambled on his belly through the curtain. The girl's screams and the reports of the pistols roared in his ears. The alley door. Maybe the police had forgotten to guard it.

Preston pushed the door open and looked around the gravel lot. No one in sight. Preston's car was waiting. He sped up the alley, turned the corner, and was in the clear.

Preston was worried about being followed but he got home in no time. He hid the car in the garage and ran into the kitchen. Good. His wife wasn't home yet. The gunshots and the girl's screams were still ringing in his ears.

He hurried down the basement stairs into a small room he used for a workshop. He cleared a spot on the cluttered workbench and spread a clean rag. He put the metal tablet in the center of the rag and drew some of the liquid into the eye-dropper. His heart was beating fast and he was panting.

He suddenly realized that he had forgotten to ask the girl at the jeweler's how the test fluid worked. Too late now. He'd just have to try it and see what happened. If it really was gold, he could sell it and have that secret nest egg he always wanted. Then he would be able to afford some time off to do that writing he had always been meaning to do.

Preston squeezed the eye-dropper bulb and a drop the size of a tear fell on the metal plate. His heart fluttered when he thought he saw the drop change color. When he examined the spot more closely, there was nothing there, as if the tablet had absorbed it.

He tried another drop. It had the same inconclusive effect. He became concerned that he might not be doing the test right.

Preston put the eye-dropper down and picked up the metal plate and the bottle. He poured the remaining liquid over the plate with a sweeping motion. Again he thought he saw a flicker of color as the liquid disappeared. He was almost frantic when the plate for another moment appeared unchanged.

Then as he watched and trembled, the surface of the plate took on a deeper sheen and began to glow with an intense light. Preston's breath rattled raggedly in his throat. His blood roared in his ears. Had he ruined it? Maybe it wasn't gold after all.

The plate began to crumble in his hand. One tiny piece fell on the rag. Its glittering facets caught the light. Then another fell, and another. The tiny pieces cascaded onto the floor like wheat spewing from an augur. The tablet finally disappeared completely, and Preston was left standing up to his knees in a pile of tiny glittering objects that covered the floor of the room.

He bent over and picked up a handful of the objects and carefully examined them. Even though he didn't have his glasses, he could see them perfectly. They appeared to be tiny letters of an alphabet he didn't recognize. They glittered in a haphazard jumble in the light of the naked basement bulb.

Preston looked with wonder at the delicate curves and lines and angles of each perfect letter. They were so beautiful! They had to be gold!

"I've got to hide this stuff before my wife gets here,"

Preston thought, "or the police." He had forgotten about the police. Surely it wouldn't be long before they tracked him down. He didn't want to explain where he had gotten all this gold.

He struggled to free his legs from the pile of letters but it had become like mud or tar. He began to feel light-headed and dizzy. He was sweating. He felt so tired. The empty eye-dropper bottle fell from his hand and skittered across the tiles. Suddenly the room tilted and spun and the floor rushed up to meet him.

When he woke up, he couldn't remember where he was nor how long he had been there. He was lying on his back looking up at the basement bulb. His arms were extended straight out to each side of his body. Then his mind cleared and he remembered he had to hide the gold. When he rolled his head to look, the glittering pile of golden letters was gone. All he could see was the empty eye-dropper bottle in the corner.

"All that gold," he said, and stopped. Anxiety, regret, guilt, greed, fear, everything, seemed to float away from him. It was all suddenly clear and simple. "It doesn't matter," he said. "I don't have to worry about hiding it anymore."

Preston stood up. He felt buoyant, better than he had felt in years. A bright light was shining through the door of the dirty basement room. He walked into the light and never looked back.

Preston's wife was angry and unhappy when she drove home from her church meeting. Preston had let her down again. She was not going to let him off easily. When she turned the corner of her block, she was surprised to find a police car sitting in her drive way.

The officer introduced herself politely and informed her that there had been an unfortunate incident involving her husband. Could she come to the station? No, the officer couldn't give her any details. Just come right away.

When she arrived at the station, a detective took her to a barren room furnished only with a small table and two wooden chairs. He offered her coffee.

"Mrs. Gault, your husband was involved in an attempted robbery at a jewelry store about an hour ago," the detective told her. "I'm very sorry to have to tell you that he was shot and killed."

Preston's wife could not believe what she was hearing. Surely, there was a mistake. Her husband was a respected university professor.

No, there was no mistake.

Mrs. Gault broke down. The detective comforted her as best he could. When she began to recover, he told her what had happened.

A silent alarm had been activated at the station at 1653 hours indicating a possible robbery in progress at Abram's Jewelry. A patrol car happened to be in the area and was dispatched immediately. When the officers arrived the front of the store was empty. They were just moving into position when a subject, a white male about fifty, unshaven and wearing ragged dirty clothing, ran at them from the back room. The subject appeared to be in a highly excited state. The subject pulled something from his pocket as he ran. The officers saw metal glint in the subject's hand and thought it was a weapon. Their weapons discharged killing the subject instantly. The subject had no ID on him. The officers traced the subject's identity and address through his car registration. The subject was Preston Gault.

"When the officers checked the subject's, your husband's hand, they found it to contain this," the detective said. "We're trying to understand what happened here, Mrs. Gault. Do you have any idea what the significance of this might be?"

As he spoke, he extended toward her his upturned palm. On it was a small red stone.

All About Love

At some point, if you're lucky,
you realize it's all about love,

that affinity of one atom, one molecule
for another, that laving of light

and air and water over
every surface of your body,

that astonishing beat of blood
through the tiniest capillary,

or one hand touching another,
keeping every cell alive.

You're lucky, too, if you realize
it is an undeserved gift,

a grace, a blessing,
yours to receive, withhold,

or give to another
and no act of will can sustain it

one second beyond
the second that wears it out.

Then all that's left is a stone
perhaps, a mark on a piece

of paper, a memory of a touch
as proof that it existed at all

and the proof itself
must be taken on faith

because it is only a stone
or a mark or a sound.

Lost and Found

Driving back from dinner at Josie's in Scammon we turn north out of Weir and immediately find ourselves on an unfamiliar gravel road that winds through a low-water ford across a creek and then crosses Highway 400, where we discover a small settlement of houses we've never seen before, no sign, no name, and after that a community center, and then every mile or so, one trailer park after another, some merely dilapidated, others abandoned or burned out, and every mile road that crosses our route, whether paved or graveled or sanded, poses a question, "Where might I lead?" but we do not turn, and, crossing Highway 126 almost unawares, we keep going north past abandoned farm houses with yards crowded with equipment rusting in the weeds and pastures scattered with cattle, always with the sense of Pittsburg somewhere off to the east, until finally, giving in to a pull that's grown stronger with every mile, we turn right, and it's then we become aware that we are traversing a large square with home at its center, and going east now we pass through another little settlement, Capaldo the sign says, and then after a jog south on 69 Highway past Moore's Furniture and the car dealerships, we take a left on McKay right down the main street of Frontenac, and even though we've been here many times before, the spell of the unfamiliar persists, and we look at the Catholic Church and Pallucca's Grocery and the bakery with something of the wonder of tourists, luxuriating so much in this sense of discovery that paints even the familiar with a tint of the new that we don't turn down Rouse as we normally would but go on east past the ball fields until we come to Free King Highway where we could turn south and end up in a few minutes right at our front door, but we look at each other and wishing still to remain under this spell of the beckoning unknown, with unspoken assent we continue east, passing more houses we've never seen before with kids shooting hoops in the driveways and men gathered around trucks with their hoods up, then a low-water concrete bridge under a railroad trestle, mile after mile after mile, until the road dead-ends at a private driveway with a gate and a large sign that says in huge red letters, THE BROCK RANCH, but which might as well declare, "We know where we are even if you don't," and forced now to turn one way or the other, and again with a glance and unspoken assent, we turn right and define another corner of this big square we've been tracing along unfamiliar roads this past hour or more, never above 30 mph, as if to say "We're in no hurry to find our way back," and going south now, but with this turning also knowing that we are no longer resisting the pull of home, we continue to look with a sense of awe at the strip pits, the wooded sloughs and streams, an abandoned farm, the house and barn, if they exist at all, so totally overgrown that only the metal tops of three silos glint among the treetops to indicate what a once thriving enterprise it was, crossing more mile roads to who knows where, until finally we emerge at the boarded up Fisca station on Highway 126, right on the Missouri line, and we linger at the stop sign and look across at the gravel road that disappears invitingly over a slight rise a quarter mile or so ahead, and almost reluctantly, but again with unspoken assent and even a certain relief, we turn west now, having found what we didn't even know we were looking for, toward the comfort of familiar ground and home.

Tailpiece

From the top strand
of the barbed wire fence
bordering the road
the elegant scissor-tail,
pearly gray phantom
perched in horizontal profile
above wind bent pasture grass
and ditches deep in wildflowers,
of a sudden launches a display
of daunting loops and dives,
flaunting with arrogant grace
in the face of all mere
earthbound mortals
that impossible length
of forked tail.

Stephen Meats was born in LeRoy, Kansas, and raised in Concordia. He attended Kansas State University before transferring to the University of South Carolina in 1965 where he earned his bachelor's (1966), master's (1968), and doctoral degree in English (1972). He taught at the Air Force Academy and the University of Tampa before coming to Pittsburg State University in 1979, where he is currently Professor of English. At the University of Tampa he served as Chair of the Humanities Division (1974-1979), and at Pittsburg State as Chair of the English Department (1979-1985, 1990-2009) and as Interim Dean of the College of Arts & Sciences (1983, 2009-2011). Besides scholarly articles, editions, and reviews, Meats has published one book of poems, *Looking for the Pale Eagle* (1993). His poems and stories have appeared in numerous journals, including *Kansas Quarterly, The Quarterly, Tampa Review, Arete: The Journal of Sport Literature, Hurãkan, Flint Hills Review, Prairie Poetry, Dos Passos Review, Angel Face,* and *The Laughing Dog*, and in the anthologies *Kansas Stories* (1989), *Begin Again* (2011), and *To the Stars Through Difficulties* (2012). He has served as poetry editor of *The Midwest Quarterly* since 1985. He lives in Pittsburg with his wife, Ann, three Boston Terriers, seven cats, and six hives of bees. (Photograph by Ann Meats)

MAMMOTH PUBLICATIONS BOOKS

* Indicates an E-Book format

Barry Barnes, *We Sleep in a Burning House,* poems, $10

Xánath Caraza , *Conjuro* (English, Spanish, Nahuatl), poems, $18

Robert Day, *We Should Have Come by Water*, arts ed. poems, $20
            We Should Have Come by Water, chapbook, $10

Diane Glancy, **Now It Is Snowing inside a Psalm*, prose, $12
            Stories of the Driven World, prose, $14
            It Was Then: Diagram of the Elemental, poems, $12

Caryn Mirriam-Goldberg, *Landed*, poems, $12

Caryn Mirriam-Goldberg, editor. *To the Stars: A Kansas Renga*, $18,
      Kansas Notable Book,

Jonathan Holden , **Glamour*, poems , $12

Denise Low, *New & Selected Poems* (2nd ed., Penthe Press), $15
      *Thailand Journal (E-book) $10, K.C. Star Notable Book
      Touching the Sky: Essays (Penthe Press), $12

Denise Low, editor, *To the Stars: Kansas Poets*, Ks Notable Book, $12

Stephen Meats, *Dark Dove Descending: Poems and Stories*, $12

Theresa Milk, **Haskell Institute: 19th Century Stories of Survival* , 20

Lana Wirt Myers, *Prairie Rhythms: Life and Poetry of May Williams
      Ward,* $14, Kansas Notable Book Award

Elizabeth Schultz, **White-Skin Deer: Hoopa Stories* (print and E-
      book), $12

William Sheldon, *Rain Came Riding: Poems*, $12

Pamela Tambornino, **Maggie's Story: Teachings of a Cherokee
      Healer*, $14 *Maggie's Story: Teachings, hardcover, $24*

E. Donald Two-Rivers, *Fat Cats, Powwows: Poems*, 2nd ed., $12

Thomas Pecore Weso, **Wisconsin Indigenous News* 1865-1930, $6

Thomas Weso & Denise Low, *Langston Hughes in Lawrence*, $12

EMAIL ORDER **mammothpubs@gmail.com** (PayPal)
MAIL ORDER: 1916 Stratford Rd. Lawrence, KS 66044

CPSIA information can be obtained at www.ICGtesting.com
Printed in the USA
LVOW07s0424100215

426400LV00001B/40/P

9 780983 799559